illustrated by Stephen Michael King

Librarian Reviewer
Marci Peschke
Librarian, Dallas Independent School District
MA Education Reading Specialist, Stephen F. Austin State University
Learning Resources Endorsement, Texas Women's University

Reading Consultant
Sherry Klehr
Elementary/Middle School Educator, Edina Public Schools, MN
MA in Education,University of Minnesota

STONE ARCH BOOKS
Minneapolis   San Diego

First published in the United States in 2007
by Stone Arch Books,
151 Good Counsel Drive, P.O. Box 669,
Mankato, Minnesota 56002.
www.stonearchbooks.com

First published in English in Sydney, Australia,
by HarperCollins Publishers Australia Pty Ltd in 2003.
This English language edition is published by arrangement
with HarperCollins Publishers Australia Pty Ltd.

Library of Congress Cataloging-in-Publication Data
French, Jackie.
    My Mom the Pirate / by Jackie French; illustrated by Stephen
Michael King.
        p. cm. — (Funny Families)
    "Pathway Books."
    Summary: When he asks his mother, a privateer for Queen
Elizabeth, to go to school she insists it be the best one in the world, only
it is over four hundred years in the future.
        ISBN-13: 978-1-59889-345-8 (library binding)
        ISBN-10: 1-59889-345-9 (library binding)
        ISBN-13: 978-1-59889-438-7 (paperback)
        ISBN-10: 1-59889-438-2 (paperback)
        1. Pirates—Fiction. 2. Mothers and sons—Fiction. 3. Time travel—
Fiction. I. King, Stephen Michael, ill. II. Title.
PZ7.F88903Mzm 2007
[Fic]—dc22   2006027146

1 2 3 4 5 6 12 11 10 09 08 07

Printed in the United States of America

Table of Contents

Chapter 1
A Pirate Crew 5
Chapter 2
Cecil's Birthday Wish. 11
Chapter 3
You Want What? 15
Chapter 4
The Wizard. 18
Chapter 5
The Problem with School 21
Chapter 6
Parent-Teacher Night. 29
Chapter 7
Mom Goes to School 32
Chapter 8
The Day After Is Even Worse. 39
Chapter 9
A Terrible Morning 42
Chapter 10
A Message from the Principal 45
Chapter 11
All Over School 50

Table of Contents
Continued

Chapter 12
Rain 52
Chapter 13
Saved From the Flood 75
Chapter 14
The End of the Black Ship 91
Chapter 15
Freedom 95
Chapter 16
Off to the Next Adventure 103
Epilogue 106

CHAPTER 1

A Pirate Crew

"I'll chop your toes off to feed to the fishes!" yelled Mom, waving her sword at the evil ship captain.

The battle raged across the decks of the pirate ship *Mermaid*.

Mom leaped down the stairs, grabbed the captain, and gave him a kick in the backside with her boot, sending him over the rails and into the water.

"Take that, snot whiskers!" Mom yelled. She peered into the coil of rope where Cecil was sitting with his books. "Is your homework done?"

"Not yet," said Cecil. "It's hard to concentrate with all the noise going on."

"I don't care. I want that homework done before bedtime," Mom called.

"Mom," shouted Cecil as she leaped back onto the bridge after another villain.

Filthy Frederick's wooden leg clattered across the deck. "Sorry, me hearty," he yelled to Cecil. "But your mom's busy!"

"A pirate's life is the way for me," sang Filthy Frederick, swinging his wooden leg.

"With lots of enemies on the sea,

With chests of treasure and jewels, too,

A fine free life for me and you!"

"Snap!" agreed Snap, peering out of the coil of rope. Snap was Cecil's pet crocodile. Mom said no one was going to grab Cecil if he had a crocodile on guard.

Cecil turned back to his homework.

Behind him, the fight was nearly over.

Ambrose One Arm and Harry the Hook were carrying treasure chests to their ship. In the sea, the evil sailors were swimming over to a small desert island.

Mom made sure there was an island nearby when she made prisoners walk the plank or tossed them overboard, and if one of them couldn't swim, she threw him a life jacket.

"Jelly-bellied sons of a sea serpent!" snorted Mom, striding back over to Cecil.

She wiped her sword on her pants.

"You lads," bellowed Mom to the pirate crew. "You want sea monster or pizza for dinner tonight?"

"Pizza!" yelled Filthy Frederick.

"Pizza!" cried Barnacle Bruce.

"Pizza!" shouted Harry the Hook.

"Make sail for shore!" Mom yelled.

Mom threw Cecil a bag of gold. "Take these down to the rare coin shop when we get to Bandicoot Creek and order the pizzas, will you? Get some of that white stuff, too. What's it called again?"

"Milk," said Cecil.

"Right," agreed Mom. "Nine gallons of their best milk, too."

Cecil sighed as he shoved his homework back into his bag.

He wished Mom and the crew had never discovered pizza.

He wished Filthy Frederick would get singing lessons.

He wished Snap could learn to use a toothbrush.

But most of all, he wished he didn't have to go to school tomorrow.

It wasn't that Cecil didn't like school. He did. He liked playing football with the other kids at lunchtime. He loved learning and reading books. In fact, that was how the whole problem began.

It started a year ago, on his birthday.

CHAPTER 2
Cecil's Birthday Wish

The whole ship had a party every year on Cecil's birthday. Cecil woke up early. He pulled on his stockings, pants, shirt, and pirate hat, and headed out into the passageway. Someone had decorated the ship with pirate flags.

"Happy birthday, son!" cried Mom, putting her tea down on the table and kissing Cecil on the cheek.

"Happy birthday to you!

Happy birthday to you!

Happy birthday, dear Cecil,

From all of the crew," sang Filthy Frederick.

The table was covered with presents. Cecil sat down and opened them.

There was a pirate ship in a bottle from Harry the Hook. A giant skull with a candle in it that Filthy Frederick had carved for him. A spoon carved out of a shark's jaw from Shark-eyed Pete. Barnacle Bruce had knitted him a bright red hat with three pom-poms, and Putrid Percival had made him a big box of chocolate sea monsters.

One last present sat on the floor. It was
an old sea chest. Mom grinned. "Aren't you
going to open it?" she demanded.

Cecil lifted the lid. "Books!" he cried. "A
whole chest of books!"

Mom grinned. "I suppose you're
wondering what I got you. Well, I was
thinking, I want my son to have whatever
he wants! So, what would you like? A chest
of treasure? A small island? A pet leopard?
Anything! It's yours!"

Cecil bit his lip. There was just one thing he wanted, one thing he wanted more than anything else. He gulped. "What I'd really like," he began.

"Yes?" said Mom.

"More than anything else . . . ," said Cecil.

"Anything!" said Mom.

"I want to go to school," said Cecil.

CHAPTER 3

You Want What?

"School!" yelled Mom. Her tankard of
tea dropped from her hand and hit Snap
on the head. (He had a hard
head, so he didn't notice.)

"Yes," said Cecil.

"But no one in our family has ever
gone to school!" protested Mom. "I never
went to school. Your dad never went to
school. We've always been pirates! Grandpa
was a pirate, Grandma was a pirate, even
Great-Granddad was a pirate."

"But I don't want to be a pirate," said Cecil.

Suddenly Mom stopped yelling. "What do you like?" she asked softly.

"I like books!" cried Cecil. "I like reading and writing and things like that."

Harry the Hook scratched his head with his hook. "Lad's right," he said to Mom. "You can't make him into a pirate if he doesn't want to be one."

"He's a reader all right," said Filthy Frederick. "Some kids are weird that way," he added.

Mom scratched Snap's back with her boot. Snap grinned happily. He loved having his back scratched.

Then Mom nodded. "So be it!" she declared. "Cecil goes to school. But not just any school! No studying with a tutor! I want my son to go to the best school in the world! We need to find ourselves a wizard!"

CHAPTER 4

The Wizard

The pirate crew had to capture three more ships before they found a wizard.

He wasn't much of a wizard. His robe looked like Mom's bathrobe and had gravy stains all over it, and someone had sat on his pointed hat, so now it was a squished and squashed hat instead.

Mom eyed the wizard doubtfully. "If you're a wizard, how did they keep you prisoner?"

"It was the iron," said the wizard. "Magic can't touch iron. As long as they had me chained, I was helpless. They were planning to sell me."

Mom looked the wizard up and down. "Well, you're free now."

"Wait," said the wizard. "I want to thank you. Wizards always pay their debts."

Mom sighed. "Okay. Let's say you are a wizard. Then there's only one thing I want. My son is more precious to me than any treasure in the world, but he likes reading. He wants to go to school. If that's what he wants, I want him to go to the best school in the world."

The wizard looked at Cecil, then he looked at Mom. Then he nodded. "Sail toward the sun for seven days," he said. "Then turn left at the next star. You'll sail through a time warp that will take you to the future. Your son can go to the best school in the world."

Mom blinked. "What's a time warp?" she asked.

It was too late. The wizard had disappeared. "Shiver me timbers! He really was a wizard!" Mom exclaimed.

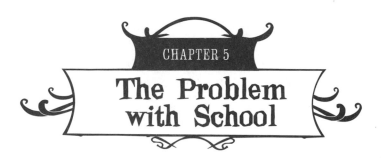

CHAPTER 5
The Problem with School

Through the time warp ten days later, Cecil was at Bandicoot Flats Middle School, two hundred years in the future. And three months later, it was almost Parent-Teacher night, and Cecil was wishing he'd never heard of school at all.

Cecil looked out the classroom window. Down in Bandicoot Cove, Mom, Filthy Frederick, and the rest of the crew waited on the *Mermaid* for him to come home from school so that they could sail back through the time warp before dinner.

It was hard just to sit in a classroom all day, after being able to roam around the ship as it sailed the seas. But school was interesting too, and that made up for it. Cecil had learned a lot in the months he'd been at school.

"Okay," said Mr. Farthingale, "your homework tonight is the problem on page thirty-six and the spelling list on page fifty-three. And remember, it's Parent-Teacher night tomorrow! It starts at eight, and there'll be tea and coffee in the library." The bell rang as he added, "Class dismissed."

Cecil shuddered. Parent-Teacher night! He could just imagine what would happen if Mom walked into the school in her boots and pirate hat and sword!

He'd thrown away the note, so Mom hadn't seen it!

There was no football practice that afternoon. Cecil sauntered out the door and out the front gate.

"Hey, CJ," yelled Shaun from the bus stop. "Want to come over? Jason and I are renting a DVD."

"I . . ." Cecil hesitated. It would be great to go over to someone's place, just like a normal kid. He'd never even seen a DVD. He shook his head. "Sorry, I can't. I told Mom I'd go straight home."

"Okay," said Shaun. "See you tomorrow!"

"Yeah. See you." Cecil walked slowly down the street. Even if Mom hadn't expected him back on the *Mermaid*, there was no way he could have gone to Shaun's house. If you went to someone's house, then they'd expect to come over to your house.

Cecil shook his head. How could you bring friends home to a pirate ship? Explaining that his name was really Cecil, not CJ, would be the smallest of his problems.

It was about a twenty-minute walk to the cove where the *Mermaid* was anchored. Cecil was just crossing the road by the pizza place when he heard a voice. "Ahoy, young fellow!"

Cecil turned. It was Filthy Frederick. He limped over to Cecil, seven pizza boxes in his hands.

"Your mom sent me out for pizza!" he explained. "I'll walk home with you."

Cecil looked around. No one from school was watching, and anyway, Filthy Frederick had taken off his pirate hat to come into town. He'd even tied back his long hair.

A few passersby looked at his wooden leg and one bare foot, or they looked around to try to find where the smell was coming from, but most ignored them.

"How was school?" asked Filthy Frederick, his wooden leg tapping as they walked along.

"Okay," said Cecil.

"Me and the crew would love to see that school of yours one day," said Filthy Frederick.

Cecil crossed his fingers. "Parents and, uh, friends aren't allowed to come to the school," he said. "It's a rule."

"Well, if it's a rule, we'd better obey it," said Filthy Frederick.

"Hello, CJ!"

It was Mr. Farthingale. Cecil tried to sink into the concrete. "Good afternoon, sir," he whispered.

Mr. Farthingale smiled at Filthy Frederick. "Is this your father?"

Filthy Frederick grinned over the pile of pizzas. "Shiver me timbers! I'm not the lad's father! No, I'm . . . "

"My great-uncle," put in Cecil. "This is Great Uncle Frederick, Mr. Farthingale. Great Uncle Frederick, this is Mr. Farthingale, my teacher."

"Pleased to meet you," said Mr. Farthingale.

"Teacher!" Filthy Frederick beamed. "Shiver me, I never thought I'd meet a real teacher! I was just saying to the lad, how much his ma and me and the boys would love to see that school of his."

"Why not come to Parent-Teacher night, then?" asked Mr. Farthingale.

Filthy Frederick frowned. "What's Parent-Teacher night?"

"It's when parents and teachers can talk about how kids are doing in class, and parents can see some of the work the class is doing," explained Mr. Farthingale. "It's tomorrow night."

"Shiver me timbers!" roared Filthy Frederick again. "The lad's ma will be there, all right! The whole crew will be there!"

No! thought Cecil. No!

Filthy Frederick nodded at his pile of pizzas. "Better get these back before they get cold! Pleasure to meet you, Sir Teacher."

Cecil bit his lip as they walked away. Mom and the crew coming to Parent-Teacher night! What could he do now?

CHAPTER 6
Parent–Teacher Night

The deck of the *Mermaid* was scattered with pizza boxes. The skull and crossbones flapped merrily in the breeze.

Mom took a last bite of her pizza. "That was the best dinner I've had since we captured the king of Spain's chef," she said happily. "Now, I'd better get myself tidied up for this Parent-Teacher night. What do you think I should wear, son? My new black boots and the lace shirt with velvet buttons?"

"Um," said Cecil. "Most of the other moms will be wearing dresses."

Mom laughed. "A dress! I'd get my sword tangled in my petticoats!"

"But, Mom, women don't wear great big skirts and petticoats any more. They don't wear swords either," he added.

"No sword?! No, son, I'd feel undressed without my sword at my side. That was the sword I wore when I married your dad and on the day you were born," Mom said.

"Mom, you don't really want to come to Parent-Teacher night! It'll be boring!"

"Yes I do!" cried Mom. "I've never seen a school before! Or met a teacher! Now, are any of you landlubbers coming to Parent-Teacher night with us?"

"Parent-Teacher night's just for parents," put in Cecil, then felt mean as Filthy Frederick's face fell.

"Snap?" asked Snap, crawling up to Cecil's feet and grinning with his giant, yellow teeth.

Cecil shook his head. He felt worse. "It's not for crocodiles, either," he said.

"Never mind, lads," said Mom. "I'll tell you all about it. Hey, why don't you pick us up afterward?" she said to Filthy Frederick. "Sail up Bandicoot Creek. Bring the crocodile, too. It'll be fun for him and will save Cecil and me from walking back in the dark. Cecil, come on. We don't want to be late."

CHAPTER 7
Mom Goes to School

The school was already crowded when Mom and Cecil arrived. The buzz of conversation stopped as Mom walked in.

"Who's that?" someone whispered.

Someone laughed. "She must be on her way to a costume party!"

Cecil led Mom to Mr. Farthingale's table. Mr. Farthingale's eyes widened as they walked up. He glanced down at Mom's sword and gulped.

"Mr. Farthingale, this is my mom."

"Pleased to meet you, Mrs. . . . ?"

Mom grinned. She thrust out her hand.
The ruby flashed in the lights. "Tanya the
Terrible. Just call me Captain Tanya."

"Captain Tanya." Mr. Farthingale
looked stunned as he shook Mom's hand.
"Please sit down. CJ has been doing
very well."

Mom beamed. "That's my boy!" she exclaimed.

"And I hope we'll see you at the football game this Saturday."

Mom frowned. "Football?"

"It's a game," hissed Cecil. "That's what I do on Saturday mornings."

"Football?" Mom's forehead creased even more. "You play it with one foot? You hop maybe? Or does the team all have wooden legs?"

"No, two feet," Mr. Farthingale said.

"Then it should be feetball!" declared Mom. "I've never been to school but even I know it's two feet, not two foots. Can parents come to these feetball games?"

"Of course. The more people the better," said Mr. Farthingale.

"Wonderful!" boomed Mom. She looked at Cecil. "Why didn't you tell me parents could come to the feetball games? The crew and I will be there, swords at the ready in case there's trouble," she added to Mr. Farthingale. "You never know when a sword will come in handy!"

Mr. Farthingale stood up. "Perhaps you'd like a cup of tea," he suggested.

"Never say no to tea," said Mom. "Best thing to come out of China since gunpowder. Thank you, teacher!"

"Thank you too," said Mr. Farthingale. He looked stunned.

Cecil quickly steered Mom over to the tea table. It was almost over now! "Look, are you sure you want a cup of tea?"

"What's your hurry, lad? The crew isn't even here yet." Mom picked up a small cup and looked at it.

"Is this the best they can do? Well, fill 'er up, son!" Mom said loudly.

"Could you speak more quietly, Mom," whispered Cecil, embarrassment crawling up from his stomach to his face as Mom clicked her tea cup against his. "You're not on the ship now!" Tea poured onto the floor, but Mom didn't seem to notice as she drank hers down.

"What use is a captain if her men can't hear her?" boomed Mom. "This is good tea, son!"

"How about a cookie?" asked Cecil. "Two cookies?" If Mom's mouth was full, she'd have to be quiet.

"Ah, CJ, I was looking for you."

Cecil turned. It was Mr. Pootle, the football coach. "I'm afraid I had to drop you from the team this Saturday," said Mr. Pootle. "You weren't quite as fast as you could have been last week."

Cecil tried not to sound disappointed. "That's all right, sir."

"What did you say?" Mom crashed her cup down on the table. The tea splashed onto the plate of cookies. "You're dropping my son from the feetball team?"

"Um . . ." Mr. Pootle looked nervous. "Just for one week, you understand."

"My son likes the feetball team!" roared Mom.

"Mom, it's okay," whispered Cecil.

"The crew and I were going to watch him next Saturday! The crew really wants to see this lad play feetball!"

Mom reached for her sword. Oh no, not the sword! thought Cecil.

Mom raised the sword high into the air. "Do you want me to feed your feet to the fishes?" she cried.

"What?" whispered Mr. Pootle.

"You'll walk the plank!" Mom cried.

"Okay," whimpered Mr. Pootle. "He's on the team. Just put the sword down."

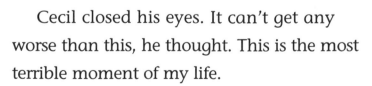

Cecil closed his eyes. It can't get any worse than this, he thought. This is the most terrible moment of my life.

But he was wrong.

CHAPTER 8

The Day After Is Even Worse

It rained the next day. The waves lapped at the *Mermaid* and the drops pounded on the deck as Cecil pulled on his school clothes.

"Fried sea monster or cereal?" asked Putrid Percival as Cecil trudged into the galley for breakfast.

"Just cereal, please," said Cecil.

"You sure? That cereal was fresh yesterday. No time to get any maggots to add flavor," Putrid Percival said.

"I don't mind," said Cecil. He wasn't hungry. If only I didn't have to go to school today, thought Cecil. If only I was like everyone else at school. If only my mom was anything except a pirate.

"Good morning, everyone," muttered Mom, stomping into the galley in her boots and bathrobe. "Tea, please." She took a drink then smiled at Cecil. "Good night last night, son," she said.

"Mom," said Cecil, "maybe it's not such a good idea for me to go to school. I just don't fit in there! Maybe I really could be a pirate."

"You still don't want to be a pirate," stated Mom. "So you have to go to school. Well, have a good day. We'll just have a quiet day scrubbing out the ship. I'll make sure Putrid here has hot sea monster soup for you when you get back."

"Thanks, Mom," said Cecil.

"Have fun," said Putrid Percival, stirring something stinky on the stove.

Fun, thought Cecil. Yeah right.

Snap watched sadly as Cecil tramped up the stairs and out onto the wet deck.

CHAPTER 9

A Terrible Morning

It was raining even harder as Cecil pulled his tiny boat up onto the beach. Water poured down the gutters as he walked up the footpath, then down the hill again to school.

Cecil walked through the school gates. He could feel the stares as soon as he entered. Someone pointed at him and giggled. He heard the word "pirate" as he turned the corner by the library.

Jason and Shaun came up to him. Jason nudged Shaun, and Shaun nudged Jason. Finally Jason said, "We saw your mom last night."

"Yes," said Cecil.

"Was she really going to attack Mr. Pootle with her sword?" asked Shaun.

Cecil tried to laugh. "No, of course not! It was just a joke."

"Mr. Pootle didn't look like he thought it was a joke," said Shaun.

"Well, it was," said Cecil. "Mom was going to a costume party afterward. It wasn't a real sword."

"It looked real," said Jason.

Cecil gave a sick grin. "Of course it wasn't real! Whoever heard of a mom with a sword!"

Jason glanced at Shaun. "I guess," he said.

"Look . . . ," began Cecil, just as the bell rang.

Cecil breathed a sigh of relief. Saved by the bell! For the first time he was actually glad!

CHAPTER 10

A Message from the Principal

The next hour wasn't too bad. Mr. Farthingale kept giving him strange looks, but at least no one said anything about pirates or swords or attacking coaches.

Cecil was hoping that maybe everyone would forget about Parent-Teacher night when one of the third graders knocked on the door.

"Message from Mrs. Parsnip," she said. Mrs. Parsnip was the school principal. "CJ, please go to her office immediately."

Cecil gulped. Mr. Farthingale looked at him kindly as he stood up. "Go ahead, CJ," he told him.

Cecil had never realized it was such a long way to Mrs. Parsnip's office. His feet seemed too heavy to ever get there.

There was a kid already sitting on the hard wooden seats outside Mrs. Parsnip's office. It was Big Bernie, the school bully. He smirked at Cecil. "What are you here for?" he asked.

"Don't know," said Cecil.

Big Bernie smirked again. "I have to sit here until the end of the period," he said, then put on a silly voice, "because I was disrupting all the others."

I bet you were, you pile of donkey doo, thought Cecil. He didn't say anything. He just knocked on the door and waited.

"Come in." Mrs. Parsnip looked up from her desk. "Ah, CJ," she said. "I'm afraid I've had some complaints about your mother."

"Oh. Sorry, Mrs. Parsnip," said Cecil. "Mom was just going to a party afterward and got a little carried away."

Mrs. Parsnip looked at him. "Waving a sword and threatening to attack a teacher is more than just being carried away."

"It was a joke!" protested Cecil.

"Well, I for one don't think it was funny. Neither did Mrs. Bumpus, the president of our parent and teacher association. In fact, Mrs. Bumpus suggested that your mother might believe she really is a pirate!"

"But . . . ," began Cecil.

"Now, CJ, of course it's not your fault if your mother is a little strange."

Cecil blinked. "My mom isn't strange!"

"Well, wearing a pirate costume all the time and waving a sword isn't exactly normal," Mrs. Parsnip said.

Cecil lost his temper. Mom might be embarrassing, but she was also the bravest pirate in the world! And she was his mom. "Mrs. Bumpus is a crazy old lady!" hollered Cecil. "My mom's not crazy! She really is a pirate! She got this wizard to send me to the best school in the world, but if he thinks this is the best school, then he's a pretty dumb wizard!"

"CJ, do you really believe your mother is a pirate?" shrieked Mrs. Parsnip.

"Yes!" shouted Cecil, "and she's a really good one."

"The sooner I have a chat with your mother, the better," muttered Mrs. Parsnip under her breath. Then she said, a little louder, "All right, CJ. You can go back to your class now, but I expect to see your mother tomorrow!"

Cecil slunk out of the office. Big Bernie smirked at him. "That was really interesting! I heard every word!"

"Oh, go feed your fingers to the fishes," muttered Cecil. He was too upset to worry about Big Bernie now.

CHAPTER 11

All Over School

It was all over the school at lunchtime. Big Bernie must have told everyone, thought Cecil.

He felt sort of glad that the secret was out. Secrets were a heavy weight to carry, and anyhow, so what if he was different? So what if Mom was different?

The rain pelted down onto the asphalt. Cecil sat in a damp corner by himself and tried to chew his sea monster sandwiches and stared at the rain.

"Hey, CJ!" It was Shaun and Jason.

"What do you want?" muttered Cecil.

"We just wanted to ask, is your mom really . . . ?" Shaun began.

"Yes!" yelled Cecil. "She really is a pirate! So go away!"

"You don't have to yell," said Shaun.

Jason nudged him. "Leave him alone," he said. He hesitated, then said, "We're eating lunch if you want to sit with us."

Their footsteps splashed across the asphalt.

Cecil didn't even look up. He didn't want to sit with anyone. He didn't want to speak to anyone. He just wanted to eat his sandwiches, but now he wasn't hungry.

Cecil threw his sandwiches away and stomped off to the library, where he could be alone.

CHAPTER 12

Rain

It rained through lunch. It rained through math.

Cecil looked at his watch. Only another hour to go and then he was never coming back to school, ever. He'd become a pirate even if it meant leaving behind the library and the computers and all the books.

And your friends, said a small voice in his brain.

They're not my friends! Cecil told himself. No one would want to be friends with a kid from a pirate ship!

He looked at his watch again. Fifty-eight minutes till the bell. Suddenly the bell rang, over and over. Then it stopped, and Mrs. Parsnip's voice came through the intercom.

"Attention! This is an emergency. I repeat, this is not a drill! Proceed immediately to the cafeteria. I repeat, this is an emergency. Everyone is to go to the cafeteria now!"

"What's happening?" asked someone in the back.

Mr. Farthingale shook his head. "No shoving, no running, just grab your bags and walk, don't run, as fast as you can to the cafeteria."

Chairs scraped as kids got up.

Cecil stood up. "What do you think is wrong?" whispered Shaun behind him. Cecil shrugged.

"Can't be a fire," said Jason. "Not in this weather."

Cecil grabbed his bag and walked to the cafeteria.

Mrs. Parsnip was wearing her raincoat and hat. "Is everyone here?" she called.

There was a chorus of yeses from the teachers.

"Then please listen carefully. There is no need to panic, but we have to move fast. The dam has burst up the river." There were gasps all around them. Someone screamed faintly toward the back of the hall. "Now calm down. The floodwaters will hit us in approximately half an hour," continued Mrs. Parsnip.

Cecil craned his neck to see out the hall door. The creek looked much the same, smooth and brown and only a little higher.

Mrs. Parsnip said, "Most of the town should be all right since it's on a hill, but the school is on lower ground, right by the creek. Emergency services has arranged for school buses to pick up everyone from school and take them to safety before the flood gets here. Settle down!" she yelled as cries and chatter broke out across the room. "I said there was no need to panic!"

She went on, "There aren't enough buses to take everyone at the same time, so we will start with the youngest children first. Miss Appleby, could you take your class out to the bus stop, please, then Miss Lee's class and Mrs. Peter's."

Mrs. Parsnip paused, then glanced at her watch. "There is really plenty of time," she said. "All right, I want everyone to stay in their seats until the buses come back, but you can talk among yourselves."

Cecil sat frozen in his seat as the excited talk buzzed around him. A burst dam! A wall of water rolling down the river! Had anyone else in this room ever seen a giant wave? Did any of them know how powerful water could be?

Jason nudged him. "Better than math, anyway."

"Yeah. I suppose," said Cecil, frowning.

"You okay?" asked Jason.

"Yeah, I'm fine." Cecil looked at his watch. How long would it take for the buses to take the younger kids to safety, then come back and take them, too?

Ten minutes passed and the buses still hadn't come back. Fifteen minutes. The water would be thundering toward them.

Mrs. Parsnip's cell phone rang. She answered it, spoke briefly, then put it away. "The buses are on their way back," she announced.

Everyone headed out the door. Some of the kids were laughing, but others looked worried.

Cecil walked alone, his hands in his pockets. The rain was even harder now.

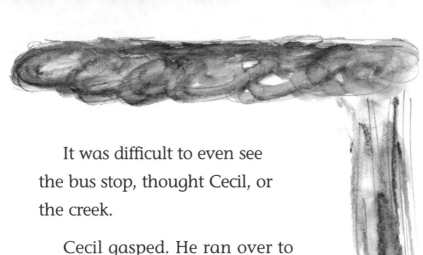

It was difficult to even see
the bus stop, thought Cecil, or
the creek.

Cecil gasped. He ran over to
Mr. Farthingale. "Sir! Sir! The
creek! It's rising! Look!"

Mr. Farthingale peered at the
creek through the rain. The little
creek had vanished. The water
swirled, brown and frothy, over
the banks.

Every second it rose higher
and higher, eating the banks
in great hungry gulps. The
ground disappeared.

Mr. Farthingale took one glance at the deserted road and bus stop, then made a megaphone with his hands. "Everyone back to the cafeteria! Now!" he yelled.

"Why should we?" began Big Bernie.

Cecil turned on him. "Don't you know how to obey orders!" he yelled. "You wouldn't last five minutes on board a ship!"

Big Bernie smirked. "Your mom's pirate ship? Hey," he said to Jason, "did you hear? This guy thinks his mom's a pirate."

"I bet your mom's a baboon," said Jason. "That's how she got a big baboon for a son. Come on!"

Cecil glanced back. The water was still rising up the hill. It was almost at the basketball courts now.

What was Mr. Farthingale thinking? The cafeteria would be flooded in a few minutes. They'd be trapped inside!

"Okay," yelled Mr. Farthingale. "I want everyone up on the roof. Mrs. Parsnip and I will help you. Shaun and Jason, you go first, then you can reach down and help the others up."

Jason climbed up, then reached down to help Shaun.

"No way!" Big Bernie shoved his way to the front and elbowed Shaun out of the way. "I'm going next! I'm not waiting for the flood to get me!" He looked back nervously. The football field was under water.

Mr. Farthingale looked like he might protest. He caught Mrs. Parsnip's eye. She shrugged. It was quicker just to help Big Bernie up.

Big Bernie's feet disappeared over the edge of the roof. Jason leaned down to grab Shaun's hand, then Shaun and Jason leaned over to help more kids.

Cecil waited. No matter how scared he was, he wasn't going to push his way to the front like Big Bernie. He'd let the others go first.

"Snap!" What was that? Cecil looked around. It had sounded like . . .

"Snap!" The crocodile chewed a hot dog and stared at him from under the garbage can.

"What are you doing here, you dumb crocodile?" yelled Cecil.

Snap stared at him.

Cecil bit his lip. Snap must have followed him to school! He must have been worried about him and swum up the creek.

"Crocodile!" squeaked Mrs. Parsnip. "Is that a crocodile? There aren't any crocodiles in Bandicoot Creek!"

"Get back, CJ!" yelled Mr. Farthingale. "That thing looks dangerous!"

"He's not dangerous!" explained Cecil. "He's a pet!"

"A pet crocodile!" Mrs. Parsnip protested. "We don't allow pets at school!"

"Come here!" yelled Cecil again. Snap blinked at him, confused. "Hurry!" screamed Cecil. The water was halfway up to his knees. Snap didn't move.

"CJ! Up on the roof! Now!" shouted Mr. Farthingale.

"I can't leave Snap," cried Cecil.

"CJ, the water's rising fast!" shouted Mr. Farthingale.

Snap thrashed his tail in the water. "Snap?" he asked. He sounded worried.

"It's all right, boy," called Cecil. The flood swirled around Cecil's knees. He could feel the water tug. "Swim over to me, Snap!" he cried. The water tugged at Cecil's waist. "We'll both drown if you don't come," shouted Cecil.

Suddenly Snap moved. One minute he was cowering in the water, the next he was swimming through the water and leaping up onto Cecil's shoulder.

"Ow!" cried Cecil as twenty pounds of crocodile tail and bad breath landed on him. He began wading back towards the hall, with Snap hanging over his shoulder like a wet crocodile-skin towel.

The current pushed and pulled at him. He'd never make it! The water was too high, the current too strong.

A strong hand grabbed his. "You'll be all right!" yelled Mr. Farthingale above the noise of the water. He pulled Cecil through the floodwaters back toward the school.

"Hurry!" shouted Mrs. Parsnip, eyeing Snap. She held Mr. Farthingale's other hand in hers, steadying them both as they forced their way through the flood.

Mr. Farthingale hoisted Cecil, complete with crocodile, up onto his shoulders. Up on the roof Shaun and Jason leaned down, their hands reaching for his.

Snap grunted in Cecil's ear, his claws digging even deeper into his shoulder, his jaws reaching up to Jason and Shaun's hands.

"Don't bite their fingers off, you dumb crocodile," yelled Cecil. "They're trying to help us! This is no time for a snack!"

Snap closed his jaws. Jason and Shaun each grabbed one of Cecil's hands and pulled him.

Up, up, up. Cecil's wrists felt like they might break with the weight of his body, and Snap's, too.

Then suddenly he was on the roof, gasping and trying to catch his breath.

Shaun and Jason pulled up Mrs. Parsnip as Mr. Farthingale pushed her up from below.

"Umph!" said Mrs. Parsnip as she landed belly down. She looked up. "Everyone stay away from that crocodile!" she ordered.

"He won't hurt anyone!" gasped Cecil as Snap crawled off his shoulder onto the roof. Someone screamed, but Cecil was too tired to care.

Suddenly a hand shook his shoulder. "CJ, we can't reach Mr. Farthingale!" yelled Jason above the noise of the flood and rain. "There's no one down there to help him get up here!"

Cecil hauled himself upright, staggered to the edge of the roof, and peered down. The water was almost up to Mr. Farthingale's shoulders now. "Can't he climb up part of the way?"

Jason shook his head. "There's nothing to hang on to!"

Cecil thought fast. When you came aboard ship, you climbed the ladder, and if there was no ladder, the crew sent down a rope. "Quick!" he yelled. "Take your coat off! Fast!" Cecil stripped off his own coat.

He grabbed Jason's coat, then Shaun's, and twisted them together with his own and knotted them.

"What are you doing?" yelled Jason, above the noise of the flood.

"Making a rope! One coat wouldn't be strong enough, but if I tie a few together, they will be."

Cecil threw the coat rope down to Mr. Farthingale. Mr. Farthingale grabbed it.

"Jason, hang on to the rope on my left," Cecil yelled, "and Shaun, you hang on to the right. Now everyone get behind one of us and hold on to the person in front like a tug of war. When I say pull, pull!"

The class lined up behind them.

"Pull!" yelled Cecil. "Mr. Farthingale, jump!"

Mr. Farthingale jumped. For a moment his legs dangled in the water, then, slowly, they dragged him up.

"Ouch," said Mr. Farthingale. He landed on his tummy on the roof.

"Snap?" said Snap. He crawled onto Mr. Farthingale's back and sat down.

"Get off, you dumb crocodile," gasped Cecil, shoving him off with his foot. "That's a teacher, not a pillow!" Suddenly his legs wouldn't hold him anymore. He collapsed down onto the school roof.

Snap crawled over to him and put his snout in Cecil's lap.

"Hey, is that crocodile dangerous?" asked Jason.

"No," said Cecil. "Well, a little," he added. "He does eat bad people. He chews their fingers and toes, anyway."

"What's going to happen now?" Big Bernie looked down at the raging water. He seemed to have gotten smaller in the last hour.

Mrs. Parsnip tried to smile. "There's nothing to worry about," she said. "I'm sure the flood won't get higher. And if it does, well, someone will rescue us!"

"How?" demanded Big Bernie. "There isn't any boat around here big enough to take us all!"

"Yes, there is," said Cecil.

Big Bernie rolled his eyes. "Oh, yeah? Your mom's pirate ship, I suppose?"

"Yes," said Cecil.

"Huh," said Big Bernie. "Just because you've got a crocodile doesn't mean you've got a pirate ship, too! Who believes in CJ's pirate ship?" He looked around triumphantly.

Immediately Jason and Shaun put their hands up.

Cecil blinked. "Hey, thanks," he whispered.

Then slowly Mr. Farthingale stood up and put his hand up too. He grinned. "Listen," he said.

Suddenly everyone on the school roof was quiet. The only sounds were the beat of the rain and the crash of logs and sticks as they hit the walls, and . . .

"With a yo ho ho and you'll walk the plank." It was Filthy Frederick, singing!

"The deck was slimy, the galley stank,

The porridge smelled of seagull doo,

The briny deep's too good for you!"

"Here they come!" yelled Cecil as the
Mermaid sailed across the brown and
boiling water.

He ran to the other end of the roof. "Hey, Mom!" he yelled as he waved his arms. "We're over here!"

"Ahoy, shipmate!" yelled Harry the Hook from the crow's nest. "The captain heard on that radio thingy you bought her for Mother's Day that you were having some trouble up here! Thought we'd see if we could lend a hand. Or a hook!" he added.

Mrs. Parsnip sat down suddenly in a puddle on the roof. "It is a pirate ship!" she whispered.

Big Bernie blinked. "Is that a real sword?"

"Hey, cool," said Jason. "They're flying the skull and crossbones!"

"Look at all those sails," cried Shaun.

"Hi, Mom," said Cecil.

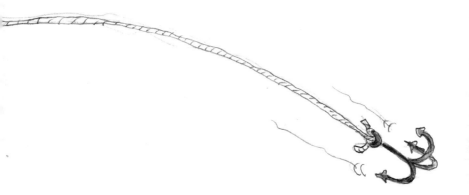

CHAPTER 13

Saved from the Flood

The good ship *Mermaid* slowed down next to the school.

"Step lively," ordered Mom, marching up and down the deck with her hands on her hips.

The kids climbed onto the ship.

Cecil handed Snap to Filthy Frederick.

Snap looked relieved to be back on the ship. He crawled over to a pile of rope, lay down, and shut his eyes.

Mom strode up to Mrs. Parsnip and held out her hand.

"Captain Tanya the Terrible, at your service," she said.

"I'm Mrs. Parsnip," said Mrs. Parsnip.

Mom beamed. "Then you're the school principal," she cried. "The captain of the school, right?"

"Yes," said Mrs. Parsnip.

Mom nodded. "Tell me, Lady Principal, do you make the kids walk the plank, or do you put them in the school dungeon?"

"Um," said Mrs. Parsnip, "usually detention."

Big Bernie nudged Cecil. "Does your mom really put people in dungeons?" he whispered.

"No, of course not," said Cecil. "Mom is totally against dungeons."

Big Bernie breathed out again. "Of course. I knew she wouldn't," he began.

"She just makes them walk the plank," said Cecil.

Big Bernie turned pale. Cecil grinned. He didn't think Big Bernie needed to know that Mom only made people walk the plank if there was an island nearby.

Mrs. Parsnip looked pale too. Mom patted her arm. "Why don't you let Putrid Percival make you some tea?" she suggested, "and maybe a bowl of hot sea monster soup, too."

"Thank you," said Mrs. Parsnip. "Not the soup. I'm sure it's delicious, but no thank you."

Suddenly she turned green and ran for the side of the ship.

"Seasick," said Mom. "Shark-eyed Pete, fetch the lady some of Cecil's seasickness potion. Maybe you'd better get her a bucket, too. Now trim the sails, you scurvy mongrels!" she yelled to the rest of the crew. "Let's get this ship going!"

Mom grinned at Mr. Farthingale. "We'll have you back on dry land before you know it."

Jason looked at Mr. Farthingale. "Sir, do we have to go back to dry land now? Couldn't we go for a sail? Just a little one?"

"Well, you'd have to ask the captain," said Mr. Farthingale.

Mom beamed. "It would be fun," she said. "Head her out to sea and through the time warp, boys!"

"Time warp?" asked Mr. Farthingale.

Mom nodded. "That's how Cecil gets to school. The wizard showed us." She grinned.

The *Mermaid* changed course.

Soon the land was distant. The rain had eased to a gentle drizzle, but the clouds hung low.

Then all at once the light changed. The air turned blue, then green, then gold. You could almost hear the air sparkle.

Suddenly the air was clear again. The rain was gone, and the land behind had vanished too. The sun beamed down from a cloudless sky.

"Wow!" yelled Jason. He ran to the rail. "We're out at sea!"

"And back in the past," Cecil told him. "No computers, no phones. Just sailing ships and sea monsters!"

"Look there, Captain!" cried Harry the Hook. "By thunder! It's the *Black Ship*! She's headed this way!"

"The *Black Ship*!" Mom ran to the *Mermaid*'s rail. "The *Black Ship* is the biggest evil ship in all these waters!" she told Mr. Farthingale. "If only we could catch her! But she's too fast for us. As soon as she sees us, she runs away."

Mom shaded her eyes. "Yes, she's going about. We'll never catch her, lads."

"But you can't just let her get away!" cried Mr. Farthingale. "We have to try!"

"No use," said Mom. "Don't think we haven't tried before. But she's bigger than the *Mermaid*, with more sail."

Mom shook her head. She went on, "They can blow us out of the water while we dare not use our cannon, for fear of hitting the prisoners onboard, too."

"Wait a minute," Cecil said.

Suddenly Cecil had an idea. He stared at the big ship on the horizon.

"You said she was headed this way?" he asked.

"She was." Mom nodded.

"But she turned around when she saw us?" Cecil asked.

"That's it," said Mom.

"So if we weren't here, she might head this way again?" Cecil went on.

"Yes," Mom said. She continued, "What's wrong with you, lad? Has all that reading made your brain slow?" Mom looked at Cecil and smiled.

"No, Mom, listen!" insisted Cecil. "Why don't we go back through the time warp! Then we can wait till you think the *Black Ship* has had time to get here, and zap out through the time warp again and grab them!"

Mom said nothing for a moment. Cecil's face fell. "You don't think it would work?" he asked.

Mom nodded slowly. Suddenly she grinned. "You're a genius, lad! Why, it's enough to make me take up reading too!" she cried. "Well, almost," she added. "Filthy Frederick! Take us back the way we came! Hurry!"

"Aye aye, Captain," called Filthy Frederick.

One minute, two minutes. Suddenly the light changed again. The rain drizzled around them as the coast appeared once more.

"We need to wait ten minutes, I think," said Mom, glancing up at where the sun would have been if the clouds hadn't covered it.

Suddenly Mr. Farthingale looked worried. "The kids!" he said. "I can't take them hunting evil sailors! You have to drop them off where they'll be safe!"

"But there's no time!" cried Mom. "We'll lose her again!"

Jason and Shaun ran up to Mr. Farthingale. "We want to get the *Black Ship* too!"

"Um," said Mr. Farthingale.

"Everyone who's frightened, go below!" yelled Mom. "That okay with you, teacher? Everyone who has the stomach for a fight, grab a sword!"

There was a buzz of excitement on the deck. No one left.

"Swords!" yelled Jason. "Cool!"

"Are you sure it's safe?" said Mr. Farthingale.

Mom grinned. "No. Life isn't safe! One minute you can be safe on your ship, and next minute a typhoon can sweep you into the sea, or a sea monster swallows you whole. But while there's breath in us and life, let's live it! And help others live it too!"

Then Mr. Farthingale grinned back. "Hand me a sword!" he declared.

"On second thought," decided Mom, "maybe you landlubbers better try swords some other day. I don't want anyone cutting off hands and feet accidentally! Let's go with plan number two! Putrid Percival!" she yelled.

"Yes, Captain!" shouted Putrid Percival from the galley.

"Bring up the buckets of old sea monster guts!"

"Aye aye, Captain!" cried Putrid Percival.

"Sea monster guts?" asked Mr. Farthingale. "How do you fight with sea monster guts?"

"You'll see!" said Mom. "As soon as I yell 'Jump!' all of you jump onto the *Black Ship* and hold on to the rail. Got it?"

"Got it!" yelled the students.

"Buckets of bubbling guts coming up, Captain," called Putrid Percival.

Putrid Percival, Filthy Frederick, Barnacle Bruce, and Ambrose One Arm lugged buckets of guts up onto the deck.

"Haul them up! That's right, boys!" Mom glanced up again to where the sun should be. "Well, lads, and lasses, too, of course, this is it. Everyone get ready! Everyone obey orders!"

"Aye aye, Captain," yelled six pirates, twenty kids, and a teacher.

"Back through the time warp!" yelled Mom, waving her pirate hat in the air.

Gold light, green light, showers of sparkles, then blue sky again and white waves.

"The *Black Ship* ahoy, Captain!" shouted Harry the Hook from the crow's nest.

It was the *Black Ship*, looming up only feet away from them.

It was so close Cecil could hear as the prisoners cried with sadness, locked in the ship's prison.

The ship was so very big and so very black, with cannons poking out of every window. But there was no time now for the *Black Ship* to aim their cannon.

"Get the ropes and hooks!" shouted Mom. "Don't let her get away! Cecil, into the coil of rope!"

"No way!" shouted Cecil. "I'm fighting too this time!"

"But you hate being a pirate," began Mom.

"It's different now!" declared Cecil, and somehow it was. Somehow being with your friends made all the difference.

"Swing your buckets!" called Mom.

The pirates grabbed their buckets and threw their contents with all their might. Sea monster guts rained down on the *Black Ship*'s decks, green and bubbling.

The captain of the *Black Ship* looked
up from the wheel and stared. "Where
did you come from? What's this muck? It
stinks! Magic!" he roared, picking rotten
sea monster from his beard.

"No magic, you black-hearted varmint!" shouted Mom. "Or not much anyway," she added. "Take that, you rat-whiskered man!"

Mom leaped over the rails of the good ship *Mermaid* and onto the deck of the *Black Ship*. Cecil started to go after her but Filthy Frederick held him back. "Not till Captain says, matey. Always obey orders."

"But . . . ," began Cecil. He shut his mouth. Orders were orders.

The *Black Ship*'s captain shrieked. He raised his sword and charged down off the bridge and onto the slippery deck. "Men!" he screamed. "Attack!"

The evil sailors ran toward them.

"Arrk!" cried the first one as he saw the guts oozing over the deck. "That stinks!"

"Now!" bellowed Mom.

The crew of the *Mermaid* swarmed over the rails: six pirates with their swords, twenty kids, and a teacher.

"Now hold on to the rail," shouted Filthy Frederick, "just like the Captain told us to."

The pirates and students and teacher clustered at the rails of the *Black Ship*, as the sailors poured down from the upper deck toward them, holding swords.

CHAPTER 14

The End of the Black Ship

All at once the *Black Ship* began to tilt with the weight of the kids and the pirates and the *Black Ship*'s crew, who were thundering toward them. As the decks tilted, the evil sailors stepped in the slimy, slippery sea monster guts.

"They're all sliding overboard!" yelled Jason, holding tight to the rail.

"Yep!" said Mom, one boot on the *Black Ship*'s captain's back. She kicked him. "Off with you too, matey!"

Mom gave him a shove and he slid down into the sea.

"I can't swim!" yelled the *Black Ship's* captain, paddling and splashing.

"Oh, throw him a life jacket, someone," said Mom, stepping down off the bridge and onto the deck.

"Mom!" shrieked Cecil. A final, unseen sailor had crept along the bridge, just above her, his sword in his hand. "Don't touch my mother, doggie dribble!" he roared.

Whump!

Cecil grabbed the sailor's knees and brought him down onto the slimy deck.

"A perfect tackle!" yelled Mr. Farthingale.

Mom grinned. "Thanks, son. Looks like you learned something from all that feetball."

"Okay, that's the last of them," said Mom briskly. "Now I want everyone hauling up buckets of water to clean this deck."

"Why?" asked Jason.

"Because it's the prisoners' ship now," said Mom. "They deserve better than messy decks. The Queen wants her treasure — and we take some too — but the real business here is freeing the prisoners. With a ship to sail home in and a share of the treasure, they'll be safe and free."

CHAPTER 15

Freedom

One by one the prisoners ventured out on deck, blinking in the sunlight: kids with big eyes, women with scared, silent faces, men who had been chained.

Mom watched them from the deck of the good ship *Mermaid*. She wiped away a few tears with the big hanky with the skull and crossbones embroidered on the corner that Cecil had given her for a Mother's Day present. "Well, at least they're free now."

"Ahoy, Captain!" Filthy Frederick
hailed her from the *Black Ship*. "A couple
of the men here are sailors. One says he's
a master map reader. They'll be safe on
their own."

"Good speed to them!" called Mom.
"Now bring over our share of the
treasure!" She turned to the kids. "Half the
treasure for the prisoners, a quarter for
Good Queen Bess, and a quarter for us."

"Only a quarter?!" protested Jason. "That's not very much."

"Wait till you see the treasure," said Mom.

The pirates carried the treasure on board.

"Eight chests of jewels," said Cecil, making a note on his list, "two hundred and forty gold bars, one hundred and sixty bolts of silk, sixteen chests of pepper — pepper is worth more than gold in London," he told Jason and Shaun, who were standing nearby. "Eighty-eight barrels of cinnamon bark. That's worth even more than pepper."

Mr. Farthingale blinked. "You must be millionaires," he whispered.

Mom shrugged. "Who counts? We've got a good ship and a good life and good friends. Who cares how many chests of gold are back home in the attic? Now, let's take a look at this treasure."

Mom hauled ropes of pearls and diamonds out of the chest. "Must be something here that's suitable for youngsters," she muttered. "Ah, here we are. Choose what you want from these. And here, Sir Teacher, this is for the school." She tossed him a bar of gold.

"Wow." Mr. Farthingale nearly dropped it. "It's heavy!"

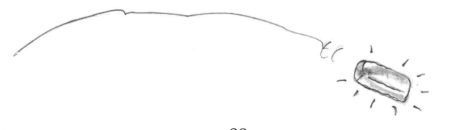

"Gold is heavy," said Mom. "Use it to buy more feetballs or books or something. And this is for you." She tossed him a sword. The jewels in its hilt flashed in the sunlight. "Anytime you want a lesson in how to use it," Mom said, "just let me know."

The kids crowded around. There were piles of rings, their giant diamonds glowing even in the shade of the sails, gold cat brooches with emerald eyes and daggers with sapphires and gold.

There were ruby buttons, gold cups with yellow diamonds around their rims, small boxes made of pearls and silver that played strange songs when they were opened, jeweled birds that sang when you pressed their golden tails, and a big wide vase that was copper outside and gold inside.

"One of each for everyone," said Mom.

Big Bernie looked up from the treasure. "The prisoners get stuff like this too?"

"Yes," said Mom gently.

"So they're rich?"

Mom nodded. "They deserve to be, after all they've gone through," she said.

"But why do they do it?" cried Big Bernie. "The evil guys, I mean. Why would they catch other people and make them prisoners?"

"Because they can," said Mom. "Some people think that if you're strong enough to do something you can just go ahead and do it. They don't wonder if it's right or wrong. They just don't think at all."

Filthy Frederick's wooden leg clattered across the deck. "Mrs. Parsnip's fast asleep, Captain," he reported.

"Ahem," coughed Mr. Farthingale. "I think I should be getting the kids back."

"Don't worry about that!" boomed Mom, slapping him on the back. "Remember the time warp?!"

"Yes, but," began Mr. Farthingale.

"How do you think we get Cecil to
school on time every day? We just think
of what time we want it to be when we go
through the time warp, and it is."

"So," Mr. Farthingale worked it out.
"We can stay here in the past as long as
we like and still get back before anyone
starts to worry?"

"Exactly," said Mom.

And so they did.

CHAPTER 16

Off to the Next Adventure

Shark-eyed Pete was showing kids how to sail, and Filthy Frederick was teaching the others his favorite songs.

"Yo ho ho it's the life for us,

As grand as a pimple all full of pus.

A pirate ship's more fun than a bus!

It's a pirate's life for us."

Cecil leaned on the railing with the wind in his face. Someone coughed behind him.

Big Bernie leaned on the rail beside Cecil, with Shaun and Jason on his other side. They gazed out at the sea.

"Hey, look! Dolphins!" cried Jason.

"They're playing in the wake of the ship," said Cecil. "They like the waves we make behind us. Dolphins really like our ship."

"And whales?" asked Shaun.

Cecil nodded. "Ambrose One Arm says he saw a mermaid once, too."

They watched the dolphins grinning as they dove in the spray.

"So your mom really is a pirate," said Big Bernie.

"Yes," said Cecil.

"Um, I'm sorry," began Big Bernie.

Cecil waved him silent. "Forget about it," he said.

"Hey," said Jason. "How do you catch a sea monster?"

"You need the right bait," explained Cecil. "First you get a really big net."

The seagulls yelled, the wind smelled of sun and salt and, sitting on the wrinkle between the sea and sky, a small island shimmered in its ring of surf and sand.

The wind filled the white sails of the good ship *Mermaid* and carried her like a bird across the waves.

EPILOGUE

Wednesday is sports afternoon at Bandicoot Flats School. The kids can choose which sport they want to play. There's basketball on the basketball courts. There's feetball on the lawn.

Or on the good ship *Mermaid* you can fish for sea monsters or practice sword fighting. You can study twenty ways to cook a sea monster with Putrid Percival, or the care and feeding of crocodiles with Snap.

And if a ship comes sailing by, you can practice being a pirate too. Cecil's mom keeps pointing out that it's not really the same when you have the queen's permission.

Every Wednesday afternoon the *Mermaid* is packed with kids, and on the *Mermaid*, Wednesday afternoon lasts as long as you want.

Everyone agrees that Bandicoot Flats
School has the best sports afternoon of
any school around. Which makes sense of
course, because Bandicoot Flats is the best
school in the world! As Filthy Frederick says:

"With a yo ho ho and a school at sea,

With lots of adventures in piracy,

We'll capture ships and set slaves free,

We'll bury our treasure all tidily,

And still be home in time for tea.

It's a pirate's life for me!"

About the Author

Jackie French has written more than 100 books for children and adults, many of them award winners, including her 2003 ALA Notable Book *Diary of a Wombat*. French loves wombats. In fact, she's had 39 of them! She says that one of the reasons she writes so many books is to pay for the carrot bill for the furry creatures. French is a terrible speller (she's dyslexic), but a terrific writer. She lives in Australia with her husband, children, and assorted marsupials.

About the Illustrator

Stephen Michael King grew up in Sydney, Australia. When he was nine, he was partially deaf, but no one noticed that he had a hearing problem. King turned to art to communicate without using words, and eventually his illustrations won him numerous awards. He lives on an island off the coast of Australia in a mud brick house.

~ Glossary ~

anchored (ANK-uhrd)—when a ship is anchored, a large, metal hook has been lowered from it, and it cannot move

chest (CHEST)—a large, strong box

galley (GAL-ee)—a ship's kitchen area

passageway (PASS-ij-way)—a hallway

passersby (PASS-uhrs-by)—people walking nearby

petticoat (PET-ee-kote)—a thin garment worn under a dress or skirt

skull and crossbones (SKUHL AND KROSS-bohnz)—the famous pirate flag, which has a black background and white bones

tankard (TANK-uhrd)—a big drinking glass, similar to a large coffee cup

time warp (TIME WORP)—in fantasy and science fiction stories, a time warp is a magical passageway between two times

ᑐᣞ Discussion Questions ᣞᑐ

1. Why are the kids mean to Cecil when they meet his mom? How should they have acted? If you met someone who was different than you, how would you act?

2. Many pirate stories involve cruel and evil pirates, but Cecil's mom and her crew aren't mean. What are some other pirate stories you know? How do the pirates in those stories act? What makes them different from the pirates in this book?

3. Cecil tells people at school that his name is C.J. Why does he do that?

❧ Writing Prompts ❧

1. Have you ever been embarrassed by someone in your family? Write about that time. What did you do about it? How did it make you feel?

2. The wizard tells Captain Tanya about a time warp that will take the *Mermaid* to a school. If someone told you about a time warp, where would you want it to take you? Write about it, and draw a map, too!

3. Create your own pirate ship. What is it called? Who is the captain of the ship? What are the crew members like? Draw a picture of your ship, and be sure to include the pirates!

Internet Sites

Do you want to know more about subjects related to this book? Or are you interested in learning about other topics? Then check out FactHound, a fun, easy way to find Internet sites.

Our investigative staff has already sniffed out great sites for you!

Here's how to use FactHound:

1. Visit *www.facthound.com*

2. Select your grade level.

3. To learn more about subjects related to this book, type in the book's ISBN number: **1598893459**.

4. Click the **Fetch It** button.

FactHound will fetch the best Internet sites for you!